THE TALES OF
SCUBA STEVE

ISFJELL POINT

STEVEN KAMLET

Fulton Books
Meadville, PA

Published by Fulton Books 2023

ISBN 979-8-88731-629-1 (paperback)
ISBN 979-8-88731-630-7 (digital)

Printed in the United States of America

FOREWORD

When I think back to my earliest days as a diver, many adventures jump out. Among these, I helped *Sea Hunt*'s Mike Nelson rescue his hapless buddy Jim from countless dive dilemmas, with a submersible robot team stopping a renegade U-boat that was tormenting beachgoers, and alongside James Bond, I took down *Thunderball* villain Emilio Largo. It's fortunate that our country club swimming pool harbored so much misadventure and international intrigue because these escapades helped shape my life's direction and build a career around my passion for diving. It's my prayer and hope that as someone who helps design and implement diver training programs, in four decades, I've paid it forward in some small way, helping others enrich their lives with a passion for seeking adventure and saving the ocean.

If you've yet to see it yourself, *Isfjell Point* (and the other Scuba Steve adventures) opens your eyes to the wonder, fascination, and adventure of the underwater world, but also its peril. This is why I've been so delighted to read *The Tales of Scuba Steve*—now in its third story—and I'm sure you will be too. As you might imagine, I totally relate to Ben's adventures, and I can picture him as an adult returning to the poles to relive and build on his *Isfjell Point* journey. I can see Scuba Steve and his friends alongside as divers, scientists, and explorers furthering our understanding, preservation, and restoration of the oceans. And I know that hundreds—hopefully thousands—of rising-generation Scuba Steve readers will see this too, imagine it for themselves, and launch careers, adventures, and initiatives that continue to benefit the future of the seas, humanity, and the world.

Author Lewis Carroll said, "Imagination is the only weapon in the war against reality." And history shows it is the most world-shaping force there is. Thank you, Scuba Steve, for helping equip tomorrow's divers and ocean guardians so well.

Karl Shreeves
Educational Content
Development Executive
PADI (Professional Association
of Diving Instructors)

A LOOK BACK

In case you missed it or forgot where we left off, here's a quick review of what happened on the first two days at Camp Oneega.

On the first day, Ben returned to camp and was excited to reunite with his friends, Oliver, Al, Danielle, and Ava. When they find out they're in Scuba Steve's swim group, they were excited to see if the rumors of fun and games were true. That's when it all begins; ending up in Hawaii at Honu's Reef, they experience undersea adventures with the local sea turtle while helping to rebuild the coral reef.

Upon arrival on the second day, Ben wonders if what he thinks happened a day earlier really did happen, but when he learns that the others were wondering the same thing, he knows it must be true.

They once again get to swim, leave Camp Oneega, and end up in a mysterious place known as Carcharodon Island, where they get caught up in some trouble. They spend their time helping free some animals from discarded ghost nets.

Now you're all caught up, so dive right in!

THE ARRIVAL

When the camp bus pulled up in front of my house, I ran to get on, but the doors weren't open. Instead, Ms. Jennifer put out the *stop* sign, turned on all the blinking lights in all colors, shut the engine, opened her door, and stepped off. Walking past me with a big grin, she went right up to my front door and knocked seven times; you know the rhythm. Mom answered and came outside to say hello. While I was talking to the others through the bus windows, Mom and Ms. Jennifer spoke. I was too far away and couldn't hear what was being said, but I can tell they both kept looking over at me, sometimes smiling, sometimes laughing. Uh-oh, this can't be good.

When Ms. Jennifer and Mom were finished talking, she walked slowly past me and got back on the bus. She proceeded to start the engine before finally opening the doors. When I climbed on, she gave me a wink and a smirk and quietly said, "I hope you learned your lesson." Again? Really? A lesson? Just like yesterday, I wonder what lesson, and when will I learn it? Will I know?

Arriving at camp, Ms. Jennifer made an announcement that not everyone was going to get off at the front of camp, but some of us were to stay in our seats so we could be dropped off at the back gate. If you haven't figured it out yet, when she said some, she meant me. I was the only one on the bus going to the back gate.

We drove around to the back, and when we arrived, Ms. Jennifer opened the door and wished me luck. Weird, right? Well, it's just camp, so what could really happen? I hopped off and looked around. Mr. Stu was waiting with the others under Sunny, the old weather tree. Ava and Danielle were playing hopscotch, Al was trying to climb the tree, and Oliver was nowhere to be found, as usual. We called and called for him, but just like always, no Oliver. Scuba arrived and was speaking with Stu when Oliver jumped from high in the tree. He landed right behind Stu, screaming, "Boo!"

WEATHER

It was very amusing, watching Stu jump. He jumped higher than Sunny. We all laughed, including Scuba Steve. All, that is, except Stu. He wasn't laughing, he wasn't smiling; he was red. We weren't sure yet if it was from embarrassment or anger, but red he was!

Once the color in his face returned to normal, Stu told us why he was having a special meeting with us. As the best swimmers in camp, he needed us to set an example for the others. He told us that the pool heater is broken and that the pools were going to be cold—very cold, almost like ice water. He wanted us to know first and somehow make it fun so the others will go in for instructional swim. He added, "One more thing. Oliver, come with me. You're going to get even colder because of your little stunt."

A few minutes later, Stu took Oliver for a walk to the kitchen where he handed him a heavy jacket and gloves, showed him the big freezer, and told him it needs to be organized so he can do inventory. Oliver put on the jacket, put on the gloves, walked into the freezer, and walked right back out. "It must be zero degrees in there!" Oliver screamed.

Stu screamed back, grinning. "Not at all, not even close. It's minus twenty-six degrees! Now get back in there, and clean it up." And with a more devilish grin, he continued, "And it must feel even worse than usual since it's almost ninety-five degrees outside."

After only a few minutes in the freezer, Oliver was able to tell that lineup was starting, so he ran out and went straight to the field just in time to see the raising of the flag. Everyone was laughing at him, and after thirty seconds, he figured out why. It was summer, hot and humid, and there he was, wearing a big winter coat, gloves, and a hat (complete with pom-pom.)

Lineup was now over, Oliver was sweating, and it was time to get to swim and get this day really started.

14

HEADING TO SWIM

On the way to swim, Danielle and Ava kept teasing and touching Oliver's pom-pom. "Hey, Ollie! Looks like you have a snow cone on your head!" said Danielle.

Ava added, "I'd like a blue raspberry if ya got one!" That got a chuckle out of everyone. Everyone that is, except Oliver.

When we got to the pool area, Oliver, Al, and I went to the boy's locker room, while Danielle and Ava kept walking to the other side to get to the girl's locker room. Al decided to grab Oliver's hat and throw it up into the rafters of the locker room, causing a wrestling match to break out before anyone was able to get changed and ready for swim.

Once the fighting stopped, Oliver tried to climb high enough to grab his hat, but no matter how much he stretched and leaned, the hat remained just out of reach. While he continued to try, the rest of us got changed and headed out to swim. Oliver followed, wearing his big coat and gloves, still sweating and still upset about the hat.

Scuba Steve began taking attendance, smirking as usual. Most days, he doesn't count us present for swim unless we're in bathing suits and ready to,

you know, swim. Today, however, was different. He walked over to Oliver and quietly asked him if he was hot. When Oliver responded with a loud and resounding "yes," that's when it happened. Scuba finished attendance, carefully put down his clip board, took off his hat, and in a very calm and deliberate manner proceeded to tackle Oliver into the pool, including his jacket and gloves. It drew the

attention of what felt like the entire camp, and they all came running to the pool fence, campers and counselors alike.

In typical Scuba Steve fashion, once he surfaced in the pool, he went right into his lesson for the day, acting as if nothing happened and would be curious as to why everyone was clapping, hooting, and hollering around the pool area. And just like any other day, any other swim lesson, the rest of us listened and followed instructions, while the rest of camp went back to their activities.

SWIM

Like yesterday, Scuba had us begin by practicing different kick styles. Everyone grabbed a kickboard and started kicking their way across the pool, everyone but Oliver. Oliver was struggling to take his jacket and gloves off. As Danielle was approaching the wall, she commented, "At least you're not sweating anymore, Ollie!" and she passed her kickboard to Oliver and told him to try swimming in his clothes.

Ava found watching Oliver trying to swim in his jacket and gloves very amusing. Despite his best efforts, he was flopping and splashing about, struggling to keep his head above water. He almost looked like a bird that can't fly, lots of flapping with little success. Joining the rest of us watching Oliver struggle to stay above water, Scuba Steve felt it was important that he doesn't drown, so he went over to help him.

With everyone back on the side of the pool, finished with practicing their kicks and out of their jacket and gloves, Scuba Steve explained what today's lesson would be. "We're learning how to make a PFD, or a personal floatation device, from our clothing. Does anyone know why we would need to do that? When could it be useful?" asked Scuba.

As expected and just like always, Oliver quipped, "When Scuba Steve tackles you into a pool. That's when it would be useful!" Everyone laughed.

"Does anyone else have an answer? I mean how often do I throw people in the pool with their clothes on?" replied Scuba Steve, adding, "Don't answer that!"

Al remarked, "What if we were fishing on the dock and a big fish pulls us in?"

Then Danielle said, "Or we're on a boat, and we hit a wave, or a whale tips us over, and we fall out of the boat."

Ava shyly muttered in embarrassment, "Or when you're on the zipline on a cruise and you don't stop like you're supposed to, ending up over the edge?"

"They were all good answers, even though most were highly unlikely. Either way, each example would be an appropriate time to have the ability to make our pants or shirt or, winking at Ollie, even a jacket into a floatation device. Let's get started," he said as he handed each of us a pair of sweatpants.

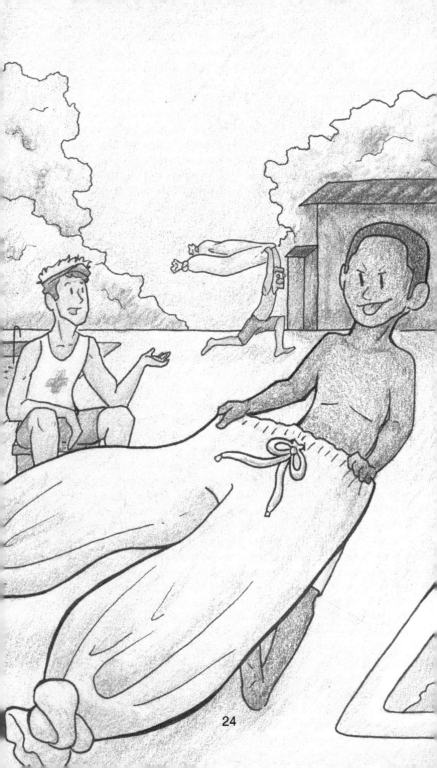

MAGIC

While everyone was practicing how to make floats out of sweatpants, Scuba Steve spoke to us about getting cold while swimming. Ava commented that if we just turn the heat on in the pool, we wouldn't get cold. Everyone else agreed and started clapping. Scuba replied by asking, "What about when you're not at camp? What about when fishing like Al said? What if you're fishing in the winter and you think you caught the big one, but it really caught you and you get pulled in?" He added, "You can tread or make your clothes into floatation devices, but you'll still get cold."

"How about wearing a wetsuit under our clothes whenever we are near water?" asked Ava.

Scuba Steve said, "That would help, and it would also help you float, but how practical would that be? Or comfortable? It would help for the time you get pulled, pushed, or fall into the water, but let's be realistic: how often will this happen? Has it ever happened to anyone you know?"

Scuba continued, reassuring each of us that we are all capable and prepared to survive should we unintentionally end up in the water, with or without a PFD. And in some instances, it's best to not have one, such as when trying to get to the bottom of the pool and touch the drain. It was at that moment Scuba Steve began pushing us in and reminding us, "You know what to do. I'll see you there!"

One by one, we all went to the bottom, and while it seemed like forever, Scuba Steve finally came in and joined us, placing his hand on the green circle on the drain.

THE TRIP

For a bright and sunny summer day, it suddenly got dark, very dark. And then just when I thought it couldn't get any darker, it did. It got so dark that it eventually got light again, but it still felt dark. This darkness wasn't black like you'd think. This darkness was blue—dark blue, light blue, everything in between and even white. Sparkling like glitter, it was darkness that shined. Despite the glitter, it was silent, and the silence was so loud, it was deafening.

The water started to get cold and noisy, making spooky popping and crackling noises like when you pour a drink into a cup full of ice. It got so cold, our eyes began to burn from the cold, and some even froze shut. Rubbing our eyes to break off what felt like

snow and ice revealed something unimaginable: giant ice cubes in all kinds of shapes and colors.

Trying to warm up, we needed to move faster and find our way to the surface. It was hard to navigate and swim through the maze of ice, trying to fit through small cracks and spaces. Eventually, we popped our heads out of the water and took a deep breath. We made it!

THE LANDING

Our breath didn't last long because it was so beautiful, it was breathtaking—the brightest blue skies and the whitest white ice and snow you could imagine. Everyone was cold, but being in the middle of the water, surrounded by ice and snow, we didn't have an idea what to do next.

Most of the ice nearby was too small for one person to climb and stand on, so Scuba Steve started swimming, and like usual, we followed. Swimming for a long time, we eventually found some bigger and bigger pieces of ice that looked like a small island. Scuba finally stopped swimming and said, "We're here. This is it!" Within seconds of telling us, Oliver tried to pull himself up and out of the water. It was not only too high, but it was also slippery and cold.

All of us were freezing cold, wet, too short to reach the top, and too weak to pull ourselves up and out. We needed a ladder, but where would we get one out in here in... wait. Where are we? Realizing we couldn't climb out and that if we stayed in the water we would freeze, we asked Scuba for ideas. Reaching his hand out, one by one, he helped each of us up and out.

Standing on the ice in our bathing suits, we were frozen and couldn't move because we were stunned at the beauty. Mostly, we couldn't move because our wet feet were actually stuck to the ice and snow.

After a few minutes of staring in awe, trying to figure out where we were, Scuba Steve told us to follow him. As we turned around, we saw a few small cabins with smoke coming from the chimneys. Where there's smoke, there's fire. Fire is hot, and we were cold. Running faster than ever before, with some of us slipping and sliding, we eventually made it inside, putting our hands in front of the fire. Best feeling ever! Where's the hot cocoa?

GLACIAL CALVING

While we were inside defrosting and getting warm, we suddenly started shaking, but not like we're cold and shivering kind of shaking. I mean we began to shake because everything around us literally began to shake—the cabin, the chairs, the tables, and the ground! *Crash! Boom! Crack!* It was so loud, I couldn't hear myself think about what was happening. The only thing I could hear was my heartbeat going *lub-dub, lub-dub, lub-dub* very quickly. I wasn't sure, but it certainly felt how an earthquake would feel.

Scuba Steve was yelling as loud as he could, but it was hard to hear what he was saying with all the noise. He came to each of us and had us move away from the windows, laying on the floor in the middle of the cabin so we wouldn't fall and get hurt by something falling from a shelf. While moving to safety, we looked out the window and saw giant pieces of ice and snow crashing into the water, causing the biggest waves I've ever seen.

Doors and windows began to rattle, eventually breaking. With glass flying all over the cabin, it's a good thing Scuba moved us to the middle of the room. Then the unimaginable happened. We started to get wet. Water started flowing through the broken windows, gradually filling the room. What now? Where will we go?

It suddenly got quiet. Water kept pouring through the broken windows. Scuba Steve carefully got up to see what was happening. He told us it was now time to move. So we got up and carefully followed him to the other side of the room where there was a closed door. When he opened the door, there was a staircase that went up, so that's what we did. We went up.

WHERE ARE WE?

"Does anyone know what just happened?" Scuba Steve asked.

Oliver answered with a resounding, "Yes! The world is ending!"

"No, that's not it," replied Scuba. "Does anyone else have an idea?"

Al chimed in and said, "Maybe there was a hurricane—"

Danielle interrupted and said, "There aren't hurricanes in cold, snowy weather."

Scuba Steve agreed with Danielle and began to explain where they were and what had happened. "As you all know, we're in a very cold place, with lots of snow and ice." He continued, "We are North of the Arctic Circle and are on ice that's floating on top of the Arctic Ocean."

We all let out a collective "Whoa!"

"Now that I told you, does anyone now know what just happened? All that noise and water flooding downstairs?"

"Maybe Pepe came back to say hello and breach. You know he makes big waves," said Ava.

Danielle added, "Or maybe it was an earthquake!"

Scuba Steve asked if anyone knew what a glacier was?

We all nodded and simultaneously said, "Yes."

He continued, "Well, we just experienced what's called *glacial calving*. Anyone know what that is?"

We all looked at him with a blank look on our faces when Oliver blurted out, "That's when the glacier gives birth to a baby calf!" Oliver then began making mooing noises like a cow. We all busted up laughing, joining in, even Scuba Steve.

After everyone settled down, Scuba started to teach us about glacial calving. He explained that glaciers are always moving. They move so slowly that you can't see or feel them move, but they're moving. Calving is when large pieces of ice break off the front end. The pieces that fall off are called icebergs, and they can be very big. Icebergs can be the size of Rhode Island. It might be small for a state, but it makes for a very big iceberg. "Sometimes, they're so big," he said, "that when they fall into the water, it can create tidal waves and tsunamis."

We just experienced calving. The end of the glacier cracked and fell off into the water, setting in motion giant waves that crashed and broke the windows, allowing water to flow and fill the downstairs rooms. We were lucky it wasn't a bigger piece of ice, big enough to cause a tsunami!

Once the water receded, we walked downstairs to see what kind of damage the cabin suffered. In addition to broken windows, wet floors, and furniture that was moved and thrown around, we couldn't help but notice something else that was left behind: Garbage, lots and lots of garbage! Bottles, bags, toys, and more were all over the place. We were in one of the most remote places on earth, and yet there was a massive pile of trash in the cabin.

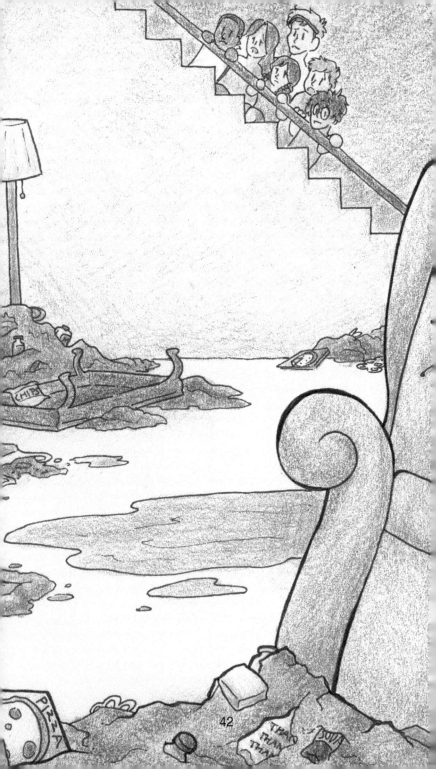

Scuba began opening every closet, cabinet, and draw. After a few moments, he yelled, "I found it! Everyone, come over and take one." That's when he handed each of us a trash bag and asked us to pick up and clean all the garbage in the cabin. There was so much trash that we kept filling our bags and had to get new ones. Hours later, when all the water was gone, we finally finished cleaning. Thirty-nine bags of garbage! Staying at camp seemed like the better choice today. We were tired, wet, and cold. Most of all, we were hungry!

Scuba Steve saw the look on our faces and told us to go upstairs and find dry clothes like sweatpants to change into while he "whipped up dinner." He began looking in the kitchen, grabbing the ingredients for what he called "his specialty." Scuba can do a lot of things, but right now, we were really hoping he can actually cook.

WHY ARE WE HERE?

About an hour later, we heard a whistle and Scuba Steve screaming, "Buddy, check! I mean, come an' get it!" Hesitantly, we all found our way to the kitchen, and boy did it smell good. On the table, was a big pot of mac and cheese and pitchers of lemonade, iced tea, and water. It seems like Scuba can cook. The mac and cheese was a great choice to get warm.

With cheese sauce all over his face and macaroni falling out of his mouth, Scuba asked if anyone was able to tell him why we're here in the Arctic.

Al was the first to answer and said, "To show us that the camp pools aren't really that cold after all and are in fact heated?"

"Nope, but you make excellent points," replied Scuba as he wiped his face. "Anyone else want to guess?" he asked. The room was silent, although I'm not certain if it's because no one knew the answer or because Scuba Steve makes really good mac and cheese and we couldn't speak with their mouths full. Scuba Steve took a drink, cleared his throat, and began to explain the purpose of this trip. "We're really far from home, in one of the most remote and unpopulated places in the world." He continued, "Yet look at these bags of trash that came from the ocean. How is that possible?"

Danielle commented that it did seem weird and that she's glad we were able to help clean up, even if it was a bit scary at the time. "Why is there so much garbage here if there aren't a lot of people?"

Scuba Steve agreed that it was scary when the glacier broke apart and the water came crashing into the cabin. He told us that most of the people up here in the Arctic are scientists who care about and are trying to find ways to protect the environment so it's unlikely the trash is from them. He then asked if anyone knows where the trash may be coming from.

No one was able to answer since everyone was so busy stuffing their faces.

"Raise your hand if you heard about a message in a bottle," Scuba asked.

Almost everyone raised their hand when Danielle added, "It's when a sailor gets stranded on an island and doesn't have a phone, so they write a letter, put it inside an old bottle, and hope someone comes rescue them."

Scuba said, "That's correct, mostly, everything except the phone part. Ocean currents carry stuff all around the world, and if you were stranded and sent a message in a bottle, you hoped someone would find it. Most ocean currents move in a gyre. Anyone know what that means?"

Oliver blurted out, "Giant. It means giant, like a giant wave."

"Good guess, but no," said Scuba Steve. "Anyone else have an idea what it means?" Again, there was silence. Scuba Steve explained, "*Gyre* means whirling circles of ocean current. There are gyres in all the oceans of the world, and just like when you walk down the street and see garbage collecting in certain spots and corners, it happens in the oceans too. Gyres carry litter and take it where it gets stuck. Over time, it builds up. What we just cleaned and put in these bags was garbage carried by ocean currents ultimately collecting here in the Arctic Ocean." He added that there are collections of garbage twice the size of Texas and very deep.

"I'll ask again. Has anyone figured out why we're here?"

Ava answered by saying that we must be here to look for bottles with a message. "Maybe we're here to rescue someone."

Scuba Steve said, "No, I'm sorry, but it would be cool to find one of those. And unfortunately, look around. Look at all the garbage we cleaned up in this one small spot. We would have to look through a lot of bottles to be lucky enough to find one with a message."

Al and Danielle were whispering, when Al called out that we must be here to clean up the mess.

Danielle shouted, "There's no way we're looking through all these bottles. That would take forever!" Scuba agreed with a nod when Danielle let out a sigh and added, "Whew! Thank goodness."

That's when Scuba Steve told us we are not here to look for messages in a bottle and rescue someone; we are here to collect trash so the animals like Honu and Pepe don't eat the plastic. We don't want them choking, drowning, or starving to death. Collectively we all screamed in excitement to help clean the ocean and save the animals.

THE DIVE PLAN

Still sitting around the table eating our mac and cheese, Scuba reminded us that the first thing we need to do is have a plan. "Oliver, please begin."

Oliver answered with "the spoon. It's always best to eat your mac and cheese with a spoon so you can scoop the sauce at the bottom of the bowl. If you use a fork, you miss out on the best part." And that's when it happened and I saw it for the first time. Not just a drink coming out of someone's nose from laughing, but macaroni!

Once we settled down, Scuba started talking about the plan. "The first thing to remember is our buddy. We're going to be in the same buddy pairs as we've been the last

two days. What happens if we can't find our buddy?" he asked.

Al blurted out, "Look around for a minute, and if we can't find our buddy, we should ascend to the surface. Our buddy should be there having done the same thing."

Scuba had a huge smile on his face because Al was right. Scuba reviewed what happened yesterday with the ghost nets and how we needed to use scissors to cut them. "Today, we aren't going to use scissors, but we have other tools to use so we can help clean up this garbage." That's when he held up a stick with a nail on the end. "Anyone ever see one of these?" he asked.

Danielle answered and said that the maintenance staff at Camp Oneega and the custodians in school use them to pick up paper, bottles, and other garbage. She called it a "pointy pick stick!"

Scuba Steve held up another tool and Ava shouted that it's a "garbage-grabber!"

That's when Scuba began to demonstrate, squeezing the handle so the claw on the end opens and closes. "Some people use these not just for garbage but to grab stuff up on a shelf. We're using them to pick up garbage when our arms can't reach or for something that may be sharp and dangerous like a broken glass bottle or a rusty can. Each buddy pair will have one pointy pick stick, one garbage-grabber, and a mesh collection bag like we used yesterday on Carcharodon Island to collect the old ghost nets," he added. "Please be aware that you may encounter some wildlife. Who knows what animals we might see?"

Oliver looked scared and unsure but said, "A walrus?"

Ava added, "Seals!"

And that's when Danielle screamed out, "Polar bears!"

Scuba Steve said that we were all right and that we may see all of them and more.

That's when Danielle screamed out, "No, LOOK! Out the window! Polar bears, right there! And there's a baby too!"

We all went to the window and let out a collective "Awwww!"

"Very cute, but let's get back to the dive. Let's review. We will be cleaning up lots of garbage, and we will probably see lots of different wild animals we've never seen before, and the water is cold, very cold. What does that mean for us?"

I said that the cold water will make us want to get out quickly, so this may be a shorter dive than the ones we've done so far.

"That's right," Scuba said, adding, "so it's going to be super important that you pay attention to how cold you really are. If you can't tell how cold you are, it's because you're numb and it's too late. You're already too cold. Please remember that we need to perform our safety stop. Who can tell me when and for how long?"

Oliver said, "We need to stop at fifteen feet for three minutes before we surface."

Then came silence, a long, long silence until Scuba Steve screamed in excitement. "That's right! You do pay attention!" He emphasized that we can't wait until the exact moment we need to get out but that we need to be prepared and allow for the full safety stop. "Please, please, please remember that if our buddy needs to get out or end the dive for any reason, we end the dive. No questions asked, except of course to see if they need immediate help. We end safely, with our safety stop. Remember, no trying to convince our buddy to stay longer. We can discuss what happened during our surface interval before the next dive, *if* there's a next dive."

"We do have a new piece of gear for cold water diving," Scuba said while holding something in his hand. "Who can tell me what this is?"

Once again, there was silence, but for a different reason. This time, no one knew the answer.

"It's a hood to keep our heads warm. It's a little weird wearing them, but it's better than being cold. I mean more cold than you have to be. If you have trouble equalizing, it's likely because of the hood. Please take your time, and make sure your ears don't hurt. Equalize early and often. Any questions? If not, let's get geared up. Pool's open!"

TAG, YOU'RE IT!

While we were getting geared up, including hoods, Ava and Danielle began laughing so hard, they slipped and fell on the ice and snow. Rushing over to help, Al asked if they were okay. That's when they laughed even more, pointing toward Oliver. Remember the hat Mr. Stu made Oliver wear in the freezer back at Camp Oneega? Well, Oliver's scuba hood also had a pom-pom. All geared up, it was time to get in the water.

One by one, we did a giant stride and splashed in. And one by one, each of us let out a loud scream when we touched the water. "It's so cold!" "It's freezing!"

Everyone had the same kind of response, everyone except Danielle. "At least it's not as cold as the pool at camp."

Once we all were in and floating at the surface, Scuba handed out the pointy pick sticks and garbage-grabbers, pointed at each of us, and flashed the thumbs-down sign to descend. First it was Danielle and Ava, then Oliver and Al, and me and Scuba. Then out of nowhere, we saw massive streams of bubbles—bubbles to our left, bubbles to our right. We were surrounded. Something kept falling out of the sky. We were lucky not to get hit or hurt. Once the bubbles stopped, the water became clear, and that's when we saw it. Seals! So many seals, big and small, they were swimming all around us.

The water was so clear, beautiful, and full of seals and fun that for a moment, we forgot how cold we were. It seemed like we could see forever, and the snowy white icebergs made it so bright down below, we could use some sunglasses. There was one problem, and that's why we were there: the trash—bottles, cans, toys, plastic bags, and even toothbrushes. They were everywhere. Now it was time to get to work.

Poking and grabbing, grabbing and poking—there was so much trash we didn't know what piece to pick up first. As we were collecting garbage, the seals were trying to eat the plastic bags. So each time we saw that happen, we pulled it away and put it in the collection bags. Most of the seals did everything they could to avoid us and stay away, all except one. The smallest one seemed to be curious and followed us around.

Everywhere we went, it went too. Al decided to try and play tag with it; he poked it on his back and swam away quickly. The seal seemed to know how to play and chased Al all around, forcing Al into a corner where he seemed trapped. It then started doing flips and spins, seemingly having a great time. Then the seal appeared to poke Al and quickly dart away. Al was stunned and realized it was his turn to chase. Let's just say Al was never able to catch the up until it turned around and came back.

While Al and the seal played around, we continued to clean until our bags were full. With all the excitement, the dive seemed to go so quickly, but within moments of each other, everyone was hanging at fifteen feet for their safety stop before surfacing with bags full of trash. At the surface, Scuba had a big smile on his face and told us that it was time to get out, dry off, and warm up with hot chocolate and cookies inside the cabin. As we got out of the water, Scuba took our garbage bags and dragged them to the cabin.

SURFACE INTERVAL

"You, guys, were awesome!" Scuba said. "Did you see how much trash we just pulled from the ocean? If we stopped now, we would have made a huge difference. But we're not stopping. We're just getting started!"

Once everyone was inside, Scuba Steve started handing out cups of hot cocoa and cookies. Eating, drinking, and talking about the first dive, we couldn't believe how much trash was in the ocean and how much we left behind. While we ate, Scuba began to exchange our tanks with full ones for the second dive.

Danielle was shaking, but not like she was cold and shivering. This was different. She had a grin on her face and suddenly blurted out, "The cookies are yummy, and so is the hot chocolate, but what about the cute seals! Are we going to talk about that? Are we?"

Everyone chimed in about the experience, and after a few minutes of listening, Scuba started to talk. "What a great surprise, and cute too! There's so much to talk about and so many questions yet to be answered. I think it's best if we start at the beginning. Anyone know why they joined us in the water? Al? How about you? You seem to have developed a special bond. Did they tell you?" Everyone started to laugh and tease Al that his best friend is now a seal.

Oliver said that it was time for free swim, just like at camp, and they obviously wanted to play. "Al's swim buddy is a seal!" Oliver said.

Ava added that maybe they were hungry for lunch.

Danielle switched it up and said, "Maybe they weren't hungry *for* lunch but were trying not to *be* lunch."

Scuba responded with, "It could be all of that, but we won't know." "Danielle, who would eat a seal?" he asked.

Danielle answered, "A hungry polar bear! Like the ones we saw earlier."

Scuba confirmed what Danielle said was a possibility and maybe the seals were trying to protect themselves. "While in the water, does anyone know why they were only trying to eat the plastic bags and not any of the other garbage?"

No one answered.

"Well, they like to eat small fish, crustaceans, and jellyfish."

That's when Ava proudly screamed out. "They must think the bags are jellyfish! But if they eat the bags, it can kill them. They can suffocate, or they can have their stomach blocked, preventing them from eating and eventually starving to death."

Scuba gave Ava a high five.

"Last but not least, we need to speak about that game of tag. It all started when Al poked the seal and swam away. Supercute, I know, but it's not a good idea to touch the wildlife, any wildlife. We don't know how they will react. If they get scared, they can attack and hurt us. Not only can they hurt us, but we can hurt them with our germs, causing them to get sick." Scuba then asked, "Are there any times it's okay to touch an animal?"

Danielle answered, "When we're trying to help, like when Pepe was stuck in that driftnet on Carcharodon Island."

Scuba had the biggest smile on his face. "Great answer, Danielle!"

"Al's new buddy needs a name. Any ideas?" Scuba Steve asked.

Oliver asked what kind of seals they are.

Scuba replied, "Great question. Did you notice the markings on its fur? The rings? They're called ring seals. The scientific name of one type of ringed seal is *Pusa hispida saimensis.*"

Upon hearing that, Ava suggested, "Saimia. Let's name it Saimia. It's pretty."

Everyone agreed.

The sun was getting lower in the sky, and it looked like it would get dark soon, so Scuba told us to hurry and finish our snack so we can gear up and get back in the water.

UNICORNS

With each new dive, we became more and more familiar with our equipment, so putting it on was starting to become easier, except we had a new problem: cold, wet hoods.

"Hey, Scuba!" called Ava. "A little help over here! Please?"

"Of course, I'll be right there," replied Scuba.

When Scuba got to Ava, he noticed she was having trouble tucking and fitting her hair into the hood. As soon as she put some in on one side of her head, even more came out on the other side. Scuba pulled and stretched the hood, while Ava and Danielle stuffed and pushed her hair up underneath. It took almost half an hour, but we were eventually successful. "Okay, everybody, the delay is

over, so let's hurry and get in the water before
it gets dark. Pool's open!"

Two by two, we all went in, descended,
and found that once again, we weren't alone.
Saimia seemed to be waiting for us to come

back. While we began collecting trash and putting it into the bags, Saimia seemingly kept trying to get in the bags too. She went from bag to bag, seeing if any of us would actually allow her to get in (or not notice if she did)!

Something was different. She didn't seem playful; she seemed skittish and scared. Danielle poked her and swam away, trying to get her to play tag, but Saimia wasn't interested. Oliver tried too, but he was also left playing alone. And that's when it happened.

It suddenly became difficult to swim. Kicking as hard as we could, we were still going nowhere, like running on a treadmill. The water got rough, pushing and pulling us everywhere, up and down, side to side. We had no control on where we were going. Trying to grab onto anything and everything, Ava lost grip of both her bag and her pointy pick stick. Bubbles, garbage, and even Saimia swirled around us. Ava's pointy pick stick flew right by Oliver, just missing his head. Whew, that was close! It missed his head, but it didn't miss his wetsuit. Like a giant thumbtack, it fastened him to the ice.

While Scuba Steve was working his way to help Oliver, Al noticed what happened and had an idea. He jammed his own pointy pick stick into some nearby ice and held on tight. What a great idea, until the others found their way and grabbed on too. It was strong enough for one person to stay in place, but once everyone else joined in and grabbed on, it broke loose. Once again, everyone started to get thrown around, everyone except Oliver and Scuba Steve.

Looking down, it began to get darker. Then the darkness started to get closer, like shadows coming up from below. Closer and closer they came; it was very strange. They had a weird shape, like something out of a fairytale. They were big and fat, but not like Pepe the whale. And there was a big stick-like horn or elephant tusk coming out of its head. If I didn't know better, I would say it was a unicorn, but they don't live in the ocean. And they're not real, are they?

Finally, they swam close enough for us to see. Unicorn whales! The whales came over to us and seemed to copy Al. Pushing their tusk into the ice the same way Al used his pointy pick stick, the whales stayed motionless. I don't know why, but the whales let us know they wanted to help.

One by one, we grabbed onto the closest tusk, preventing us from being thrown around. Scuba Steve was with Oliver who was still pinned to the ice and unable to move. As the waves subsided, one of the whales went over to Scuba Steve and helped pry Oliver away from the ice.

Once we were all together, Scuba pointed to his dive computer, reminded us to make our safety stop at fifteen feet, and gave us the thumbs-up, and we all responded in kind. This time, hanging around on the safety stop wasn't boring. We had narwhals and seals swimming all around us. Now, the water above us got dark as if someone turned off the lights. And in a split second, it immediately got bright again. From under the water, the sky was flashing like we were at a party with a DJ. It was time to surface and get out of the water.

THE AURORA

When our heads broke the surface, our regulators fell out of our mouths. We had all the air we could ever want and need, yet no one could breathe. In the blink of an eye, we were no longer cold. A warm, tingling sensation moved through our bodies. Not long ago when we got in the water, it was sunny with bright blue skies and puffy white clouds. Now it was pitch-dark and bright, all at the same time.

The sky was electric, covered in dancing flashes of blue, green, white, and pink with a background of a billion stars. It took a few minutes for Scuba Steve to convince us to get out of the cold water, partly because we couldn't hear him telling us to get out over the "Oohs and ahhs" from all of us.

When we finally climbed out of the water and got dried off, none of us wanted to go into the cabin. So Scuba went by himself and brought us the hot

chocolate, cookies, and blankets so we could watch
the light show in the sky.

While we were sitting in awe, Scuba asked, "Does anyone know what's happening?"

Ava shouted, "The unicorn whales are making rainbows! All unicorns make rainbows."

"I don't think that's it," Scuba said, adding, "but I guess it's possible. Anyone else have an idea?" While everyone was laughing and continued to watch, Scuba asked, "Has anyone heard of the aurora borealis?" A few of us seemed to mumble as if we knew, so he asked, "Has anyone heard of the northern lights?"

Suddenly, we all got louder and with excitement in our voices, simultaneously screaming, "Yes!"

Scuba Steve went on to explain that light shows like this happen near both the North and South Poles. In the north, it's called the northern lights, or aurora borealis, and in the south, it's called the southern lights, or aurora australis. He added that the lights and colors come from different gas molecules in the air. "When the molecules get charged from the sun, they light up, just like your phone will light up when charged."

GO GREEN

On the last dive, as the waves and currents got rough, we became more concerned with our safety than the trash we were collecting. Oliver had been poked by the pointy pick stick, ending up being pinned to the iceberg. We all let go of our bags trying to help Oliver or trying to not get swept out to sea.

Danielle was asking Scuba Steve if we were going to go back in for another dive so we can re-collect the lost trash when a narwhal rose from the water with a trash bag on its tusk. Scuba grabbed the bag, and just like that, the narwhal slipped beneath the surface, until it returned with another bag, and then another. This kept happening, until all bags were retrieved. Its tusk was a built-in

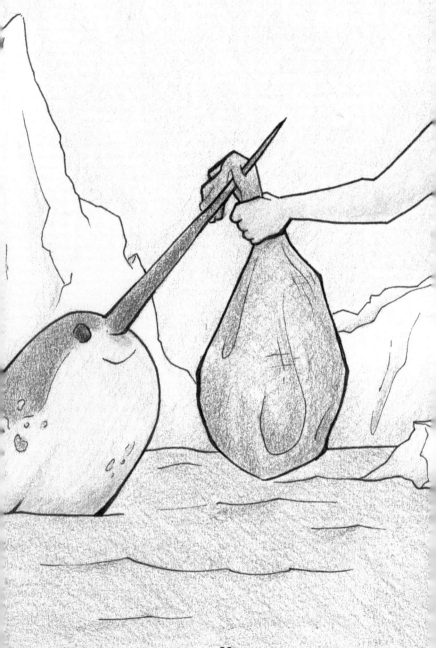

pointy pick stick, but is it possible he learned how to use it by watching us?

He was so friendly, Danielle suggested we give our other new friend a name when Scuba told us that the scientific name of a narwhal is *Monodon monoceros*. There was silence. We heard nothing except the water gently splashing against the ice when Danielle blurted out, "Donny! We should call him Donny!"

Everyone agreed and in unison began chanting, "Donny! Donny!"

And just like when the magic rainbow of the northern lights appeared out of nowhere, our new "unicorn of the sea" narwhal friend Donny appeared at the surface to say a quick hello and goodbye.

BACK TO CAMP ONEEGA

We took our garbage, placed it securely in the cabin so it can be properly disposed of, and then packed up and stored our scuba gear. We then walked on the ice and snow along the water's edge. Nothing looked familiar. When we arrived, it was bright and sunny, but now it was dark. The stars and aurora gave us light, but it still looked different and unfamiliar. On the other side of the cabin, at what looked like a random chunk of ice, Scuba Steve stopped and said, "We're here! This is our spot!" After giving us instructions, he jumped in first, and then one by one, each of us would do the same.

After we were all in the water, Scuba Steve told us to "follow the rainbow. The light from the aurora will guide us." Scuba gave a thumbs-down, and everyone responded with the same and did a surface dive. Swimming under the ice and snow was crazy. The light from the northern lights was so much brighter than what we saw while out of the water. The lights seemed to dance. The water was so full of swirling colors, trying to follow the rainbow was impossible. If we did follow it, we would just spin in circles, get dizzy, and go nowhere.

We were bumping into each other when the light seemed to stop and it started to get dark. Looking up, we saw the familiar big shape of our friend Donny and the other narwhals. They came to help. They formed a shield to block the light, making it pitch-black for just a brief moment.

Donny and his friends took their tusks, pointed them in the same direction while touching the tips, and that's when the real magic happened. Like a laser beam, all the colors formed a single white tube of light for us to swim through. Scuba pointed, instructed us to follow, and then began swimming through the light. Inside the light, it was warm, like sitting at the beach on a sunny day.

In what felt like a blink of an eye, we popped up through the drain in the pool at Camp Oneega. Surprisingly, the pool was much colder than the icy arctic waters full of narwhal magic and rainbows.

While climbing out of the pool, an old cup, straw, and some chunks of ice fell out of my bathing suit. A lifeguard yelled at me saying, "Hey, Ben! You're not allowed to bring drinks into the pool! Take your cup, and get out of the pool and off the pool deck, or I'll send you to see Mr. Stu again."

Too bad I can't tell him, but if he only knew it wasn't from me bringing a drink into the pool. Sometimes, a secret needs to remain a secret, and the only way to ensure that is to not tell anyone.

It was another crazy day at camp. Ice, snow, glaciers, tidal waves, garbage, seals, narwhals, and the aurora borealis—there's no way Mom will believe me when I try to tell her what happened. She will think I'm lying and not give me dessert once again, but that's okay because I can't wait to see what will happen tomorrow!

THE PLASTIC PROBLEM
OCEANIC PLASTICS

Every minute, the equivalent of 2 garbage trucks full of plastic are dumped into the ocean.[1] That's enough plastic to cover every foot of shoreline around the world with 5 large trash bags of plastic. This compounds each year.[2]

By the year 2050, it is estimated that there will be more plastic in the ocean than fish (by total weight.)[3]

Plastic has been found in the deepest part of the ocean at the bottom of the Mariana Trench (36,000 feet!)[4]

Over 1 million marine organisms are killed each year due to plastic pollution in the ocean. These animals often starve because the plastic prevents them from properly swallowing food.[5]

Sources:
1. https://usa.oceana.org/our-campaigns/plastic
2. https://advances.sciencemag.org/content/3/7/e1700782
3. https://time.com/4186250/ocean-plastic-fish
4. https://www.nationalgeographic.org/article/plastic-bag-found-bottom-worlds-deepest-ocean-trench
5. https://www.nature.com/articles/s41598-018-30038-z

BOTTLES & BAGS

Bottles never decompose.

They break down into microplastics between 450–1000 years. There are now more microplastics in the ocean than stars in the Milky Way galaxy.[6]

Approximately only 23% of plastic bottles are recycled, meaning 77% are not.[7]

Each year in the United States, 35 billion plastic bottles are thrown out in the trash.[7]

It takes 88% less energy to recycle a bottle than to make a new one from raw material.[7]

Worldwide, 5 trillion single-use plastic bags are used. That equals approximately 700 bags per person per year.[8]

14 bags use as much fuel as driving 1 mile.[8]

300 million per year single-use end up in the Atlantic Ocean.[8]

6. https://news.un.org/en/story/2017/02/552052-turn-tide-plastic-urges-un-microplastics-seas-now-outnumber-stars-our-galaxy
7. https://ecofriendlyhabits.com/how-many-plastic-bottles-are-recycled
8. https://trvst.world/waste-recycling/plastic-pollution/how-many-plastic-bags-are-in-the-ocean

THE ARCTIC

©Fred Greco

The arctic is the northernmost part of the earth. It is comprised of the Arctic Ocean, Canada, Russia, Greenland, Norway, Finland, Sweden, Iceland and parts of the USA.

Temps can get as low as -94°F / -70°C

There is at least one day with a full 24 hours of darkness and at least one with a full 24 hours of sunshine.

Photography has been a major part of **Fred Greco**'s life beginning in his teen years as a photo enthusiast, to his most recent forensic work conducted for law enforcement. During the in-between years, he received specialized training in aerial photography while serving in the military as a combat photographer and has owned wedding and portrait studios. His work has been published in magazines, newspapers, trade journals, and automotive publications.

Now retired, he and his wife Paula, also a photographer, enjoy traveling, taking photography to what he refers to as, "the next level." While not pursing the auroras of the Canadian Northwest Territory, the glacial expanses of Iceland or the countryside of Tuscany, Greco thrives on capturing nightscapes of local Long Island and New York City landmarks, typically including calculated alignments of sun and moonrises and sets.

Having spent time photographing in several of the National Parks, he considers what can be seen and photographed right here in America as, "food for the soul", which he believes will be feeding his passion for photography for a long time to come.

Fred's images can be seen at www.fredgreco.com in addition to daily posts on Instagram @ fgreco.images.

THE AURORA BOREALIS: THE NORTHERN LIGHTS

©Frank Olsen

This occurs when energetically charged particles from the sun collide with each other at the polar magnetic field.

This phenomenon also happens on other planets too, including Jupiter, Saturn, Neptune, Uranus and Mars.

While usually green and blue, sometimes red, purple and even pink can be seen.

Frank Olsen is a photographer living in Sortland, Northern Norway. He's been taking pictures his whole life, specializing in night/aurora photos since 2008. He has now taken more than 2 million photos of the northern lights, spending thousands of hours out in the dark and cold nights.

Living in Sortland is the perfect place for aurora photography. We can see the auroras almost every night. Here in the Arctic, we can enjoy the midnight sun during summer when the sun never sets below the horizon. On the other hand, the sun never rises above the horizon in December and parts of January.

Frank's images can be seen at www.facebook.com/VesteralenPhoto

NARWHAL
(MONODON MOMOCEROS)

©David Fleetham

Narwhal can grow from 13–20 feet long and weigh up to 1.5 tons (3,000 pounds)

Their tusk is really an elongated tooth. They only have 2 teeth.

Their tusk can weigh 22 pounds and has lots of tiny holes that allow seawater to flow through. Scientists believe it helps detect changes in their environment.

David Fleetham is one of the most published underwater photographers in the world. He began diving and photographing underwater in 1976 and has been in Hawaii since 1986. For the first ten years he photographed in the cold, but rich waters of British Columbia, Canada, and worked as a PADI Instructor and USCG Certified boat captain in various dive businesses in the Pacific Northwest and Hawaii.

David's photographs have been published around the globe, with over two hundred magazine covers to date. In 1991 his photograph of a sandbar shark appeared on the cover of LIFE. It is the only underwater image to ever be published on the cover.

His award winning work has been published by National Geographic (he has done several assignments for The NGS), The BBC, The World Wildlife Fund, The Cousteau Society, and every North American diving publication. In 2010 David's image of a manatee was selected from 50,000 entries as the grand prizewinner in the professional division of the National Wildlife Federation's photography contest. He again received the grand prize in the 2021 Colorado Environmental Film Festival Photo Contest.

David's images can be seen at www.DavidFleetham.com

OTHER WILDLIFE SPECIES

©Greg Gulbransen

The arctic region is home to many species of animals, such as polar bears, arctic foxes, walruses, seals and whales of many kinds.

These species have adapted to survive in the harsh climate with extra insulation to stay warm, white coloring to camouflage and hide, and grippy feet to prevent slipping on the icy surfaces.

Greg started out shooting fashion but transitioned over to documenting the lives of unique individuals with interesting stories. Greg loves meeting new people and tries to preserve their legacy with photography. Greg also enjoys the solace of cold weather wildlife.

His images have been published in the New York Times, Daily Mail, ELLE, Marie Claire, Harper's Bazaar, Northwell Health, The Weather Channel, Spirit and Flesh, Grazia and Pandora to name a few. Some of Greg's documentary work has been featured on the A & E Network's History Channel.

Greg's images can be seen at www. gulbransenphoto.com

ABOUT THE AUTHOR

Scuba Steve is a husband and proud father of two daughters and a puppy. Family is his first priority, but he has many interests that keep him as active as possible, including swimming, running marathons, mountain biking, and just about any activity you can think of; if he hasn't tried it, it's only a matter of time!

Known simply as "Scuba" to most who know him, it's not hard to figure out why!

As a professional scuba diver, he has been found scuba diving on five continents, dozens of countries, and many of the most remote islands around the world in all kinds of conditions: oceans, lakes, daytime, nighttime, warm tropical waters, and in subfreezing temperatures under thick sheets of ice. He has seen many things, such as beautiful fish, turtles, whales, sharks, war planes, and sunken ships of all kinds and sizes, but he continues to search for the ever-elusive sunken treasure!

Of all the things Scuba likes to do, teaching swimming to children at summer camp is his favorite. *The Tales of Scuba Steve* pays tribute to the children who have inspired him on a daily basis for the past thirty-seven summers and brings the thrill and adventure of scuba diving to everyone.

CPSIA information can be obtained
at www.ICGtesting.com
Printed in the USA
JSHW042023010623
42553JS00008B/94

9 798887 316291